P9-BBQ-514

Childrens Press International
Distributed by Childrens Press, Chicago.
1987 School and Library Edition

Library of Congress Cataloging-in-Publication Data

Mahy, Margaret.
  Mr. Rumfitt.

  Summary: To promote efficiency, an accountant bans the
seasons from his valley but finds life boring without
the changes that spring, summer, fall and winter bring.
  [1. Seasons—Fiction] I. Price, Nick, ill.
II. Title. III. Title: Mister Rumfitt.
PZ7.M2773Mh   1987   [E]   87-5103
ISBN 0-516-08988-9

Created and Designed by Wendy Pye, Ltd.

Mr. Rumfitt

CHILDRENS PRESS INTERNATIONAL

Once there was a neat man called Mr. Rumfitt who worked as an accountant. All the figures he looked at in his office added up to something, and Mr. Rumfitt thought the world should add up too. But it didn't.

"It seems to me the world is very badly run," Mr. Rumfitt grumbled.

As he went backwards and forwards in brown buses to and from work, he thought deeply about this. He decided that what was wrong with the world was the seasons.

"They are a messy way of arranging things," said Mr. Rumfitt. "The world should make up its mind what it wants and stick to it. Just as it gets hot in summer the whole thing turns around and starts getting colder until wintertime. Then it is cold. Yet is the world satisfied? No! It starts warming up again — spring, summer the whole miserable business gets underway again, around and around like a giddy roundabout. Mess, muddle-muddle and mess!"

Mr Rumfitt thumped with his umbrella every time he thought about this.

3

One day Mr. Rumfitt got tired of it all. He took his money from the bank and bought a valley, out on its own, with a house in it. He waited carefully until the seasons were between winter and spring. The trees were bare; the grass was short and tidy. The weather wasn't very hot and not very cold.

"Neat, very neat!" murmured Mr. Rumfitt, rubbing his hands in dry satisfaction. He went into his valley and built a wall around it, and hung a notice on the gate saying, 'No seasons allowed'.

"That will fix them," muttered Mr. Rumfitt.

5

So the seasons stayed away from Mr. Rumfitt and his valley. The valley was neat with leafless trees, short grass, and with neither hot nor cold weather.

Mr. Rumfitt lived a plain life there. When he had to go out of his valley to work, he read a paper all the way there and all the way back, looking at the tidy pages of black and white print and not at the rumpled seasons outside.

His smile got smaller and tighter.

Then one day Mr. Rumfitt went to the well to get water and the well was dry. This was the first surprising thing.

"This is serious," Mr. Rumfitt said. "I've no use for a dry well."

The second surprising thing was that the well answered him in a husky voice. "The trouble is there's someone sitting outside with their foot in the spring"

6

7

So Mr. Rumfitt went and looked out through his gate. There stood a girl and a boy dressed in green. Their hair was long, and the white flowers tangled in it looked like stars. Around them leaped and played a flock of clumsy young lambs.

The girl had her bare white foot in the spring that bubbled up by Mr. Rumfitt's gate. She looked up at Mr. Rumfitt with slanting, laughing, hazel eyes.

"Who are you?" asked Mr. Rumfitt suspiciously.

"Who we are doesn't matter," said the boy. "But people call us Springtime. May we come in?"

In his hands he held a flute of bamboo.

"Certainly not! No one wants you," Mr. Rumfitt said sourly.

"Your plum tree does!" the girl told him pointing.

Mr. Rumfitt looked at the bare tree by the gate.

"Is it a plum tree?" he asked curiously, and as he stared he saw the branch that leaned over the wall break into blossom.

"I'm not unkind," Mr. Rumfitt said thoughtfully. "I don't wish to be cruel to plum trees. There is no harm in just one season." He opened the gate a little. "You can come in," he said.

So in came Springtime.

9

"I will play my flute and my sister will dance," said the boy.

He leaned against the plum tree and played on his bamboo flute. It was a thin little sound but it seemed to Mr. Rumfitt that all the valley echoed with that faint piping.

The girl danced, and under her wild heels the grass grew newly green and young. She touched the trees — oh, the pink blossom! Oh, the white! The willows by the stream, the tall slender poplars, all put on their green veils.

Around the roots of the trees grew crocus flowers, purple and white, violets, white and purple, tender primroses, and tall nodding jonquils.

Across the slopes of the hill danced the Spring girl looking first like a flower, then like a tree, and then like a flame of green. Behind her lambs skipped and tossed with joy. Before her the daffodils sprang up, and so she danced with the white flock behind her and the golden flock before.

The boy ran as light as a leaf after her, and as Mr. Rumfitt stared, they waved to him and laughed at him. Then they vanished, tumbling and singing over the hill, leaving his valley bright with Spring.

11

"Oh well," muttered Mr. Rumfitt. "Seeing Spring has wormed its way in I might as well plant some cabbages."

"Who would have thought it," said the plant shop woman as Mr. Rumfitt went out with bundles of plants. "I thought he was a dry old stick, but in spring even dry old sticks get green leaves."

Mr. Rumfitt changed the notice on his gate to one which said, 'Only Spring allowed here'.

Then, one day, Mr. Rumfitt went to the well and it was quite dry.

"This isn't what one expects," he cried.

"Someone has their foot in the spring!" explained the well in its husky voice.

So off went Mr. Rumfitt to see.

There sat a man and a woman all dressed in gold with golden hair, brown skin, and amber shining eyes.

"Who are you?" asked Mr. Rumfitt.

"Who we really are doesn't matter," the man said, "but we are called Summertime and here we are. May we come in?"

"Nobody has invited you!" grumbled Mr. Rumfitt.

"Yes indeed — your cabbages have," the woman said, and she laughed. Her laughter sounded like a great bell ringing softly. At the sound, Mr. Rumfitt saw his cabbages grow fat and round and green.

"I like my cabbages to be happy," Mr. Rumfitt remarked, sounding rather grumpy but also a little bit pleased. "So I suppose I must let you in. I'm sorry my valley isn't very tidy at present, but Spring has just been through it."

Then Summertime came in and the man blew a trumpet, waking up the happy big echoes in the hills, and all the roses came into flower.

The golden woman danced and up sprang foxgloves, purple, pink and white, nodding their heads; up sprang lilies with golden hearts. With the flowers came warm scents, light, long days, hot, hot sunshine and — oh, Mr. Rumfitt's nose began to peel!

"I must buy a tent," Mr. Rumfitt thought as he waved the Summer dancers over the hill.

He bought a tent and camped by the stream. Every morning he dove into a deep clear pool and splashed like a cockabully. When he went to work Summer swam blue and gold between his eyes and his newspaper.

"That's seasons for you!" Mr. Rumfitt said, "coming between a man and serious things," but he smiled as he said it.

16

17

One day he went to the well and once again the well was dry.

"What are you up to this time?" he said.

"Someone is sitting with their heel in the spring," said the well in a husky dry voice.

So off dashed Mr. Rumfitt, sunburned and tousled, to look through the gate. There sat two gypsies, a man and a woman, both with red hair and tawny eyes, and sure enough the woman had her brown scratched foot in the spring.

"What is the meaning of that notice?" the man cried when he saw Mr. Rumfitt's long nose poke through the gate. "It says, 'Only Spring and Summer allowed in here.' We are called Autumn and we want to come in."

"Who asked you to come?" inquired Mr. Rumfitt.

"Why your apple tree, of course. Your apple tree," laughed the woman and she smiled at the apple tree.

Mr. Rumfitt saw the fruit swell and ripen under the leaves.

"Oh, well," he said, opening the gate. " I let Spring come in for my plum tree. I can't turn around and refuse my apple tree's wishes."

ONLY SPRING &
SUMMER ALLOWED
IN HERE

19

So in came rough, rosy Autumn with its tingling winds and a sudden chill in the air.

Mr. Rumfitt put up his tent under the apple tree and watched Autumn dance over his valley, watched the swirls and twirls of bright leaves beckoned down by the Autumn woman's long brown hand; watched, and munched pink and yellow apples. Autumn woman's song brought fruit to the pear tree, to the vine, to the rambling, scrambling bramble.

The Autumn man's merry violin music made the autumn crocuses come out, and marigolds as well, like cheerful little suns.

Then Autumn too, waved goodbye and went laughing over the hill.

"Well, after all," Mr. Rumfitt said to himself, "one has got to be fair, and trees need fruit as well as flowers."

He changed the notice on his gate so that it read, 'Keep out Winter'.

Then one morning he woke up in his tent and it was cold. He looked out, rough and blinking with sleep, and saw standing in the middle of his garden two tall gray people in gray robes with gray hair and gray calm eyes. Their faces were stern but their folded hands were gentle.

"Who are you?" Mr. Rumfitt cried. "Who asked you in here?"

"Who we are does not matter," said the gray man, "for neither you nor anyone will ever see our true faces. But since we are here and you are our friend, you may call us Wintertime."

"All your garden, all your valley asked us in," the woman said, "for it wants to sleep."

The flowers folded, the leaves fell, the trees grew quiet and closed in on themselves, dreaming of the time when Spring's happy piping and dancing would wake them again.

Suddenly, Mr. Rumfitt felt very peaceful with life.

"After all," he told himself, "it has been a busy year for my valley. It needs a sleep."

The two Winter people moved off as soft and gray as smoke, and Mr. Rumfitt watched them go. As they went, he said, "I seem to have wound up with the usual number of seasons and an untidy valley after all. But I'm a bit untidy myself for that matter. And I'm not sorry because now I feel sure that the seasons DO add up to something. I'm not sure what, but I feel it is a lot more than I can count to."

The gray Winter people faded over the hills and into the clouds. Mr. Rumfitt began to fold his tent.

"Spring again soon!" he told his plum tree, but the plum tree was asleep and didn't hear him.

"Then Summer!" he said to the roses.

"And Autumn!" he pointed out to the apple tree but there was no reply.

"And Winter again," he said to himself.

"Very beautiful," he murmured. He frowned at a sudden thought, then smiled and frowned all at once.

"Very untidy," said Mr. Rumfitt. But his smile was big and wide.